Brittany Figueroa
www.ScribblesnThings.com

ISBN 979-8-9887182-1-5

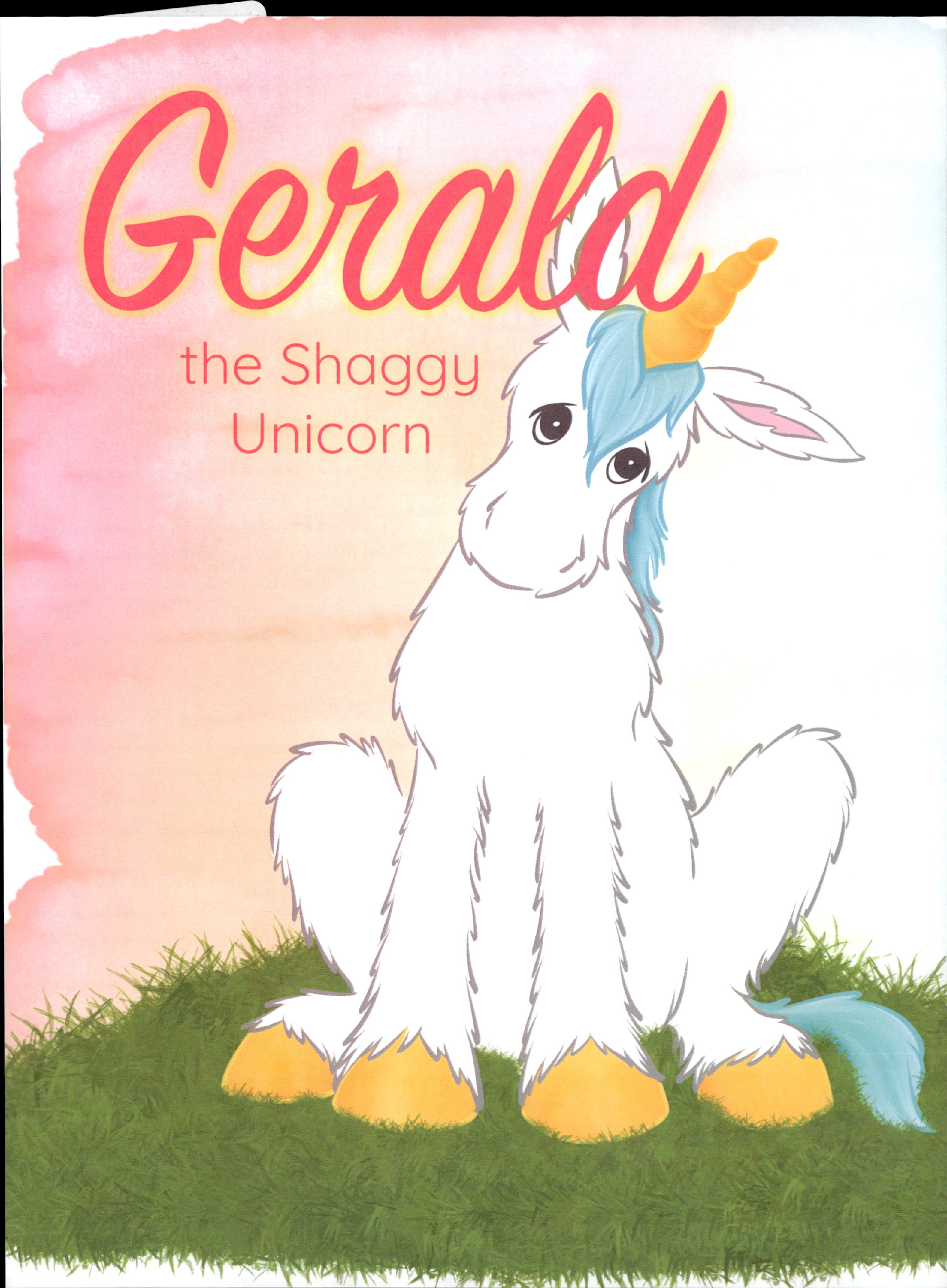

Gerald
the Shaggy
Unicorn

To all the kids who feel like they don't fit the mold, I promise you are special, just as you are. Never doubt the magic that makes you, *you*.

Sunny
Oliver
Gerald
Clay

Gerald was just another unicorn, but to anyone else, he was different. He had long, shaggy fur, unlike the other unicorns' sleek and shiny coats.

He always looked different, and as Gerald and the other unicorns grew older, they began to think that his fur was weird.

Gerald also didn't have a sparkle yet. Once the unicorns reached a certain age, their sparkle appeared. Clay, Oliver, and Sunny got their sparkle, but not Gerald. He began to wonder if there was something wrong with him. Gerald not only looked different, he felt different, too.

Occasionally, Gerald would walk up to the boys, and they'd turn away, whispering and laughing. Sometimes, they would say, "Where's your sparkle, Shaggy? Oh yeah, you can't sparkle!" Then, they would walk away, leaving Gerald feeling sad and confused.

Where's my magic? He'd wonder to himself.

He often felt very lonely, knowing they didn't want him around.

Gerald spent a lot of time alone, sitting in the meadow. One day, he wondered aloud, "I know I don't have a sparkle, and my fur is long. I don't look like the others, but why can't we be friends anyway?"

He always tried to be kind, even when others were mean. Gerald believed being kind was the most important thing, but none of the other unicorns seemed to notice that.

They only cared about his appearance and the magic he didn't have.

A little while later, a butterfly flew up and landed on a flower closest to Gerald. He noticed her wings were both different and thought they were beautiful.

"Well, hello, little butterfly!" Gerald said brightly. "What beautiful wings you have!"

"Thank you," she replied. "That's very kind of you to say. I am sometimes made fun of because my wings are different," she said sadly. "I love my wings, though, and that's what matters. My wings make me feel special, so I try not to worry about what anyone says. Even though that can be difficult sometimes."

Gerald listened as she shared, and when she finished, he replied,
"I think they're perfect just the way they are."

Harmony, the butterfly, and Gerald spent the afternoon together in the meadow, talking as the time passed. Before Harmony left, she said, "You're the kindest unicorn I've met. I will see you soon, my friend."

Gerald smiled, watching as Harmony flew away. It felt so good that Harmony saw him for the unicorn he is, and so good to have a friend!

At that moment, a warm and uplifting feeling bloomed in his heart. It spread throughout his body until it finally collected in his horn. *That was strange*, Gerald thought to himself.

It wasn't long before one of the other three unicorns looked over at Gerald and noticed something.

His horn was *glowing.*

Clay, Sunny, and Oliver immediately trotted over to Gerald. "Hey, Gerald, your horn is glowing," Oliver said, amazed.
Gerald glanced up at his horn to see that Oliver was right!

Then Sunny said, "That's interesting. I've never seen that magic before."

"Me neither," added Oliver, "that's –"

"Weird!" Clay interrupted, rolling his eyes and huffing. "Come on, guys, let's go," he said.

The next afternoon, Gerald sat, thinking, *Why is my horn glowing? Will this be another thing that they make fun of me for?*

Moments later, Harmony arrived, landing right on Gerald's nose. Seeing his new friend almost instantly made him feel better.

"Wow! Look at your new magic!" she said excitedly.

Harmony patiently listened as Gerald shared his worries.

"I think your magic is special, Gerald, just like you. It's okay if you're not like everyone else because the unicorn you are is a friend I'm proud to have," Harmony told Gerald.

Thinking about what Harmony said, Gerald decided to try to love his new magic.

A few days passed. With his horn glowing brightly, Gerald trotted proudly across the field toward where he and Harmony would meet.

Humph Clay snorted as he watched Gerald pass by. "Not only does he look different, but he doesn't sparkle like us, and now his horn glows?" he sneered. To Gerald, he yelled, "Hey Gerald, next time I need a night light, I'll come find you, and your horn can light the way!"

Oliver and Sunny noticed Gerald hanging his head. They knew it wasn't right that Clay was being mean, but they were afraid to stand up to him. He was their friend, after all, and they didn't want to make him mad.

However, this time, they noticed something else. Gerald's horn wasn't glowing as brightly as it was moments ago. It was almost as though Clay's words didn't just hurt Gerald's feelings; they hurt his magic, too.

Oliver had enough. "You know what? I think it's pretty cool that Gerald's horn glows," he stated. Clay turned back to look at his friend. "I don't think it's weird that he has long fur, and I don't care that he doesn't sparkle!"

"It shouldn't even matter," Sunny added quietly. "Gerald's always been nice, and we've been nothing but mean. Why is that?" Sunny asked.

Clay, speechless, said nothing. Instead, he watched as his friends walked away.

Gerald heard everything Oliver and Sunny said.

"We're sorry, Gerald," they said, sitting beside him. "We should have stood up for you a long time ago."

Gerald thought for a moment before responding. Finally, he said, "I bet it isn't easy to stand up to your friends, especially when they're cool like Clay. Thanks for sticking up for me this time."

Clay watched as, day after day, Gerald, Sunny, Oliver, and the butterfly would laugh, play, or hang out under a tree without him. *What's so great about Gerald?* he wondered.

It didn't take long for Clay to miss his friends. He was lonely without them and realized that this must have been how Gerald felt.

Finally, one late afternoon, Clay worked up the courage to approach everyone.

"I'm sorry for making fun of you, Gerald. I shouldn't have treated you that way. I had no reason to be mean, especially because you've always been kind." Clay looked up, hopefully, "Friends?"

Gerald looked to the others, who smiled and nodded at him.

"Friends," he replied, his horn glowing brightly.

Scan here to leave a review!

Hi there, reader!

I hope you enjoyed the story! Please feel free to share your experience or provide a star review by scanning the QR code above so that others may uncover the magic of Gerald the Shaggy Unicorn, too!

Happy reading!

Sincerely,

B. B. Figueroa

9 7 9 8 9 8 8 7 1 8 2 1 5